THE SECRET OF THE OOZE™

The Storybook Based on the Movie

TEENAGE MUTANT NINJA TURTLES II—THE SECRET OF THE OOZE

Storybook adaptation by Justine Korman
Based on the movie written by Todd W. Langen

Based on the Teenage Mutant Ninja Turtles® characters
and comic books created by Kevin Eastman and Peter Laird

Random House **New York**

Copyright © 1991 Mirage Studios. All rights reserved under International and Pan-American Copyright Conventions. TEENAGE MUTANT NINJA TURTLES® is a registered trademark of Mirage Studios USA. LEONARDO™, MICHAELANGELO™, DONATELLO™, RAPHAEL™, and all prominent characters are trademarks of Mirage Studios USA. Published in the United States of America by Random House, Inc., New York, and simultaneously in Canada by Random House of Canada Limited, Toronto. Motion picture copyright © 1991 by Northshore Investments Limited.

Library of Congress Cataloging-in-Publication Data
Korman, Justine.
    Teenage Mutant Ninja Turtles—the secret of the ooze: the storybook based on the movie / storybook adaptation by Justine Korman.
        p.   cm.
    "Based on the movie written by Todd W. Langen."
    "Based on the Teenage Mutant Ninja Turtles characters and comic books created by Kevin Eastman and Peter Laird."
    Summary: The Teenage Mutant Ninja Turtles face a new challenge when a canister of the mutagen slime that transformed them fifteen years ago falls into the hands of their enemy the Shredder.
        ISBN 0-679-81700-X (pbk.)
    [1. Heroes—Fiction. 2. Adventure and adventurers—Fiction. 3. Martial arts—Fiction.]   I. Teenage Mutant Ninja Turtles (Motion picture)   II. Title.
PZ7.K83692Te   1991
[Fic]—dc20   90-25586

Manufactured in the United States of America   10 9 8 7 6 5 4 3 2 1

From the bright lights of Broadway to the sewers of SoHo, pizza fuels Manhattan. On almost every corner window-front mozzarella technicians toss dough to the beat of boom boxes in packed pizzerias. Gallant couriers of the common slice deliver the steamy wedges through snow, sleet, gloom—and traffic!

One such peddler of pies parked his scooter and checked the address on an order slip.

"April O'Neil," teenage Keno read. She ought to buy it wholesale, he thought, lifting four boxes from the portable warmer. He stopped, hearing suspicious noises in a closed mini-mall across the street. Curiosity drew him closer.

Carrying boxes of electronics, two thugs in stocking masks crept out of the mall. They froze when they heard a voice command, "All right, hold it! You guys are under arrest."

They slowly turned and saw Keno and his pizza boxes.

"What are you, night security?" a thug sneered.

"Actually I'm pizza delivery," Keno replied. Hearing that, the thugs dropped their boxes and rushed toward him. Keno responded with a dazzling display of martial arts moves that surprised the thugs and left them unconscious.

"Did I mention I study martial arts?" cocky Keno asked.

Suddenly more thugs sprang from every corner of the mall.

"Help!" Keno gasped feebly. All the training in the world wouldn't save the

outnumbered teenager now! But he gamely took up a ready stance, prepared to go down fighting.

To his surprise, the thugs retreated!

"I must look tougher than I thought," Keno marveled.

A rousing scream shattered the silence. Swift green forms flew over Keno's head just before a drop cloth blotted his vision. Ropes pinned his arms and a voice with a thick New York accent muttered, "Sorry, kid. It's for your own good."

Keno was placed in a trash basket, listening helplessly as a fight raged around him. He struggled with his bonds. Strange voices joked above the din of battle. Who were these green guys?

"Boy, I really hate it when you thugs wear pantyhose," one said.

"You should try Sheer Energy," another advised. "Your face will feel less tired at the end of the day."

"Man, this is too easy," the New York

accent complained.

"Splinter says the true ninja is master of his environment! Stow your weapons!" commanded still another voice.

It sounded as if World War III had broken out in the mall. When he finally freed himself, Keno couldn't believe his eyes! There were four . . . what were they? Big green fighting machines. They sounded like teenagers! They looked like mutants! They fought like ninjas! They were turtles!

Keno stammered, "Who . . . wha . . . where . . . how . . ."

"Don't forget why and when," suggested the giant turtle in a purple mask, leaning on a long wooden bo.

The one in the orange mask said, "Good thing we came to see why you took so long to deliver our—"

But an elbow in the side interrupted his sentence.

"I mean, deliver April's—" Another elbow stopped him.

The turtle in the red mask said in his thick New York accent, "Look, kid. Find a phone. Call the police. We'll tie 'em up."

Keno ran to obey. When he came back from the phone booth, his masked green rescuers were gone! And the thugs hung like ornaments from the mall ceiling. The pizzas had vanished, and inside his warmer was payment and a tip.

Across the street television reporter April O'Neil returned from a long day at work. Her apartment was a mess! Not only had April just moved in, but she had several green teenage houseguests whose previous home was a sewer.

April waded through the chaos to pick up Michaelangelo's empty pizza boxes, Donatello's tools, Leonardo's chair, and Raphael's comic books. But that barely

dented the disarray.

She sighed. "The rat's the cleanest one."

No sooner had April taken the trash to the kitchen than her four friends slipped

through the living room window, each carrying a pizza box. April returned to find a fresh mess . . . and pizza for dinner again!

The energetic turtles tossed slices to each other, jumping around April's clean white furniture. No wonder her neighbors complained about her noisy "aerobics."

"So, any luck finding a new place to live?" the attractive young reporter asked hopefully. The turtle brothers shrugged.

"Not really," Donatello said innocently. "It's hard to find good subterranean housing."

Raphael said, "We can always go back to the sewer den."

Leonardo corrected him. "Yeah, right, Raph. It's a little tough when about five hundred members of the Foot Clan know where you live."

"They're all in jail. We took out the Shredder," Raphael argued from the window. "He took a swan dive into a garbage truck!" He mimed the villain's demise. "Arrrgh!"

"*Splinter* took out the Shredder," Leonardo contradicted just as their aged ninja master called from the rail of the second-story loft. Splinter was a four-foot-tall rat in dogi robes.

"Come away from the window, Raphael," Splinter said. "Never forget who you are. Ninja must always practice invisibility."

Frustrated, Raphael said, "I don't get it. We just saved the city. Why can't we—"

But before he could finish Splinter commanded, "Stand before me, my sons. For fifteen years you have been confined below. Now the outside world beckons your teenage minds, but it could never understand. That world can never be ours."

Michaelangelo raised his hand. "Not even pizza?"

The tension broke, and everyone smiled.

"Pizza's okay," Splinter said kindly.

"Man! Give a guy a heart attack," Mike said, clutching his chest as they pulled more slices from the box. April offered napkins to the greasy-fingered turtles, but was met with blank stares. She felt a headache coming on, a big headache.

"Take heart, child," Splinter said gently. "We will not be here much longer."

"Oh, no, no, no. You guys can stay as long as you want," April bravely offered. After all, the half-shell heroes had saved her life.

"Hey, cool!" Raphael said. "I kinda like—"

But Splinter interrupted. "We do not belong above."

Leonardo quickly agreed. Behind Splinter's back Raphael mocked Leo's ready obedience, which started a scuffle. Splinter intervened when the fight escalated. He ordered each turtle to do ten backflips as discipline. The brothers obeyed.

The last garbage trucks on the night shift dropped their loads into the vast pit of a landfill. When the roaring clatter had faded away, only the crickets could be heard. Then something stirred deep beneath the garbage. Soon a lone dark figure clawed to the grimy surface of a massive mound of tumbling trash.

Not far away a dozen torn and tattered members of the Foot milled about a ramshackle hut. To their dismay, they were all that remained of the once-mighty evil Foot clan.

The Shredder's assistant, Tatsu, stepped forward. With a growl the bulldog-faced ninja claimed leadership of his fallen master's followers. But a deep voice in the darkness challenged him. A shadow approached and the Foot recoiled in shock and horror.

"His face!" one gasped.

Even Tatsu was afraid as he bowed low. "Master Shredder!"

The next day in April's apartment the turtles snacked and watched her TV report. Raphael wanted to watch *Oprah*. But when he reached for the remote control, Splinter's weathered cane rapped his wrist. The ancient rat was fascinated by something on the flickering screen.

"In these days of ecological abuse," April was saying, "it's nice to find a company doing something to help. Joining me on the final day of their toxic waste cleanup is Techno-Global Research Industries spokesman Professor Jordan Perry."

Professor Perry was an old man with young eyes, dressed in a jumpsuit and hard hat. His rambling, absent-minded speech explained that TGRI, at its own expense, was disposing of its by-products in an ecologically suitable way.

"And that's really about all there is to it, Ms. O'Neil," the professor concluded benevolently.

"Thank you, Professor Perry. Reporting live from Bayonne, New Jersey, this is April O'Neil, Channel Three Eyewitness News."

A crew member gave April the clear signal and she lowered her microphone. Before she could ask any follow-up questions, the professor hurried away.

PERSONALITY PROFILE

NAME: Michaelangelo
FAVORITE COLOR: orange
FACE MASK: orange
PERSONALITY TRAITS: happy-go-lucky, wisecrackin' surf turtle
FAVORITE WEAPON: nunchaku
FAVORITE EXPRESSION: "Forgiveness is divine—but never pay full price for cold pizza."
FAVORITE FOOD: pizza
PET PEEVES: anchovies and people who don't like rock-'n'-roll

PERSONALITY PROFILE

NAME: Raphael
FAVORITE COLOR: red
FACE MASK: red
PERSONALITY TRAITS: Mr. Intensity; brooding and serious; has a tendency not to look before he leaps
FAVORITE WEAPON: sai
FAVORITE EXPRESSION: "I have an attitude?"
FAVORITE FOOD: pizza
PET PEEVES: anchovies, geeks, gacks, and people who look at him funny

"What were you going to ask him?" wondered April's new assistant, Freddy, who was busy coiling cables.

"I don't know," April said. "But don't worry about it. I'm paid to be suspicious." And she was.

Unknown to April, across the dumpsite TGRI technicians were puzzling over alarming evidence of a toxic leak.

"Grab some men," one said. "I'll go find the professor. We've got to take care of this now!"

After the men hurried off, Freddy crept out of hiding and stared at a clump of soccer-ball-sized dandelions. He fled at the approach of Professor Perry and the technicians.

"Hmm. If the soil's been contaminated this far away, there must be more leaky canisters than we thought," the professor told his nervous assistant.

"How can that be?" the assistant wondered. "They were only buried fifteen years ago."

Professor Perry shrugged. "Fifteen, fifty—just make sure the evidence is removed."

"Maybe it wasn't such a good idea to invite the press," the assistant worried.

The professor shook his head. "Sometimes the best way to hide is right out in public."

"If any of these canisters fell into the wrong hands . . ." the assistant fretted. He shuddered at the possibility.

One of the giant dandelions definitely did fall into the wrong hands—the scarred, studded hands of the Shredder!

"This isn't the reason I sent you to follow April O'Neil," Shredder scolded the frightened Freddy, who had hurried back to Foot headquarters in the junkyard. Freddy was a member of the Foot!

"But this may be even better. Whatever caused this mutation may be useful against the creatures who did this to me." Shredder studied the dandelion, bathed in the moonlight streaking through a grimy window. The armored villain was excited.

"Tatsu! Gather your best men for a mission tonight."

When April came home that night, she found a tidy tower of pizza boxes. The turtles had done a little cleaning—ninja style. Donatello wielded a mop the way he did his bo, Leonardo's katana reached those hard-to-dust areas, Raphael picked up loose garbage on his sais, and Michaelangelo's nunchaku spin-waxed the furniture.

"Thanks, guys." April smiled. "Where's Splinter?"

"He's been meditating on the roof ever since he saw your report," Leonardo told her, curious and concerned.

Then a voice spoke. "It is time. Join me above," Splinter said, surprising them all with his sudden entrance through the window.

High above the busy city April, Splinter, and the turtles sat in the evening breeze. The rat told the turtles he had spent the last hours pondering the questions of their transformation in the sewer. A light from the present now reached into the past to penetrate the veil of shadows cloaking their origin.

"The past returns, my sons. It is time to seek our answers." Splinter held up two halves of a metal canister. One half bore the initials TG; the other half was lettered RI.

April gasped. "TGRI! I knew there was something else going on with those guys." Her mind was filled with questions.

"That's the canister of ooze!" Donatello exclaimed. Fifteen years before, that same slime had changed four ordinary turtles and a rat into mutants.

"If the contents of this canister were not unique, the city faces grave danger!" Splinter warned.

Professor Perry watched a similar canister drain glowing green ooze into the complex coils and tubes of a high-tech filter in the TGRI laboratory. When only a clear liquid remained, Perry placed the empty canister on a rack with other empties and typed "disposed" on his computer.

The professor hesitated before emptying the final canister. In that moment black gloves seized him! And grabbed the last canister from his grasp.

PERSONALITY PROFILE

NAME: Donatello
FAVORITE COLOR: purple
FACE MASK: purple
PERSONALITY TRAITS: soft-spoken; full of childlike wonder; intellectual; has a knack for fixing things
FAVORITE WEAPON: bo
FAVORITE EXPRESSION: "I'm not gonna pay more for this muffler!"
FAVORITE FOOD: pizza
PET PEEVES: People who think Shakespeare is a deadly weapon

PERSONALITY PROFILE

NAME: Leonardo
FAVORITE COLOR: blue
FACE MASK: blue
PERSONALITY TRAITS: unofficial leader of the group; disciplined; calculating; cool under fire
FAVORITE WEAPON: katana
FAVORITE EXPRESSION: "Slap me three!"
FAVORITE FOOD: pizza
PET PEEVES: anchovies, bullies, and pinheads

Meanwhile, the stealthy turtles climbed from the roof of the TGRI building into a large, shadowy room crammed with computer control panels, strange chemicals, and advanced equipment. Impressed, Raphael whistled as they slinked around the high-tech lab.

"Keep on your toes," Leonardo cautioned. "It doesn't look like there's any night security, but the Foot may be afoot."

Donatello could barely contain his excitement. "So what do you guys think we'll find? You know, about us?"

"I don't know," Leonardo said.

"Whatever it is, I bet it's pretty special," Don declared.

"Yeah, either that, or we've got the wrong address," teased Michaelangelo. Donatello didn't laugh.

"Hey, Leo!" he called from Professor Perry's computer station. The monitor glowed amid the wreckage of a struggle.

"What do you make of it, Donnie?" Leonardo wondered.

"Looks like a bunch of serial numbers," replied Donatello.

Beside each luminous number was the word "disposed."

Michaelangelo shook two empty canisters he had found on a rack. "Hey, dudes!" he cried. "Like, no deposit, no return."

"Except maybe one," Donatello corrected, pointing to the last entry on the screen. Beside the final serial number glowed the word "active." The brothers huddled around the screen.

"Can you find out where it is?" Leonardo asked eagerly.

Expert Donatello was doubtful. "If the database is coded, the whole system might go down."

"Do it!" Raphael barked impatiently.

Donatello punched keys with a pencil as the other turtles watched anxiously. When he hit the final key, the screen went blank. And a lucky thing, too! The blank screen reflected Tatsu behind them, aiming his wrist crossbow!

"Look out!" Donatello yelled, diving from his chair.

The turtles ducked just before darts zipped past, shattering the screen and thunking into the walls and chair. The startled turtles found the Foot facing them. Tatsu clutched the final canister of glowing green ooze.

The turtles sprang to attack, and the brief scuffle was more like a game of hot potato than a fight. The canister was swiped, rolled, kicked, and catapulted from hand to hand almost faster than anyone could follow.

In the end Tatsu regained possession.

"Ninja vanish!" he shouted. And the Foot disappeared in a cloud of smoke.

"Hey! They're getting away!" Raphael coughed.

"Duhhhhhh!" the other turtles groaned.

The next morning April watched with a mixture of sadness and relief as the turtles packed their possessions. "But you guys haven't even found another place to live," April objected.

"It's just too dangerous to stay here with the Foot after us," Leonardo explained. He knew April would be safer with them gone.

"You know, we could go looking for the Foot for a change," hotheaded Raphael groused. "I mean, they got the ooze."

Donatello said, "First we move. Then we look."

Michaelangelo rolled up a swimsuit calendar. He rubbed his stomach. "Well, I don't know about you guys, but I could really go for some . . ."

There was a knock at the door. "Pizza!" Keno called.

"Whoa! Spookular!" Michaelangelo exclaimed.

Everyone turned to look at the door, then at Mike.

"Hey, I didn't order any," he objected.

After another knock, Keno checked to see if the door was locked. It wasn't! The turtles scrambled to hide. Michaelangelo threw a bedsheet over himself. Raphael picked up a potted plant and stood in a corner. Before April could open the door, Keno stepped through carrying a single pizza.

"Uh . . . we . . . I didn't order," April stammered, glancing around the room in alarm. Miraculously, Splinter and the turtles had vanished. She had to get rid of the curious Keno.

"Really? That's funny. The slip has your name on it," Keno said, searching the room. He picked up Mike's nun-chaku.

April snatched them from Keno's hand. "Those are mine," she asserted. "I like to do a little 'chucking in my spare time."

But April's lame demonstration left her bruised and Keno skeptical. "I'd keep practicing," he advised, studying the potted plant. Nervously April offered to pay for the pizza anyway. Keno refused, and as he turned to go, he stomped one of Raphael's exposed feet.

"*Yowww!*" Raphael shrieked, dropping the plant and hopping up and down angrily. His tender toes throbbed.

"I knew it!" Keno felt a shock of recognition as the other turtles leaped from hiding, ready for action.

"Can I hurt him?" Raphael asked. The intense turtle turned to his master and begged. "Please tell me I can hurt him. Please, please."

Keno followed Raphael's gaze to the

rat as Splinter gently advised, "I think you had better sit down."

It was raining outside when Splinter and the turtles finished their story—and the pizza. They also told Keno that there was more ooze out there, captured by a secret ninja clan.

"You mean the Foot?" Keno asked.

They were surprised he knew about the Foot. Keno told them the word on the street was that the clan was looking for teenagers with martial arts talent. Keno had an idea. "If I let myself get re-cruited . . ."

"No way, Keno," Leonardo refused.

"Hey! Believe me, I hate to say this, but the kid's got a point," Raphael argued, sharing an understanding look with Keno.

"Too dangerous," Splinter said. His word was final. Frustrated, Raphael stomped out of the room.

PERSONALITY PROFILE

NAME: Oroku Saki a.k.a. The Shredder
FAVORITE COLOR: black
PERSONALITY TRAITS: ruthless and vengeful; has a brilliant criminal mind
FAVORITE WEAPON: bo
FAVORITE EXPRESSION: "Revenge!"
FAVORITE FOOD: anything raw
PET PEEVES: Teenage Mutant Ninja Turtles

PERSONALITY PROFILE

NAME: Splinter
FAVORITE COLOR: brown
PERSONALITY TRAITS: wise; kind and gentle
FAVORITE WEAPON nunchaku
FAVORITE EXPRESSION: "Hit hard and fade away without a trace."
FAVORITE FOOD: fish eggs
PET PEEVES: The Shredder

Rain leaked through cracks in the roof of the junkyard shack. Shredder fondled the final canister in his good hand.

"It's time to find out what this ooze can do!" he told Professor Perry above the snarling and snapping that filled the room. The captive scientist put finishing touches on a crude setup of burners, tubes, and beakers. Rubber tubing snaked through a pair of small barred windows in hastily built cages.

"These were the two most vicious animals you could find?" Shredder asked Tatsu. The ninja bulldog grunted assent.

The professor stood back from his equipment. "Preparations are complete. However, I feel compelled to reregister my formal protest and remind you of the imminent dangers—"

"Begin!" Shredder commanded, and Tatsu put his grim face nose to nose with the professor's. Perry hastened to act.

"Enough small talk. Let's begin," he agreed nervously, and turned a valve that released a flow of glowing green ooze.

The muck sprayed the cages to a chorus of yelps and yowls.

April squinted through the curtain of rain pouring past her umbrella. The shadowy street was deserted.

"All clear," she reported, and the turtles scurried from her building's dark doorway to the manhole at April's feet.

Each said a simple good-bye and jumped straight down into the sewer. Except Michaelangelo, who did his Bogart imitation.

"Maybe not today, maybe not tomorrow, but soon . . ."

Mike was cut short by a swift green hand yanking him through the hole. The lid swiveled into place, and April found herself alone in the silent street. Rain drummed onto her umbrella. She missed them already.

Raphael angrily kicked a can and stopped the turtles. The brothers had spent hours searching a subway shaft for a new place to live.

"This is stupid. The Foot's up there with the ooze, and we're down here playing Century 21," rebellious Raph grumbled. "Leo! Even you can think of something better than this."

"I'm outta here," Raphael announced when Mike broke up the scuffle between the ever-squabbling Leo and Raph. He disappeared into the shadows before Leonardo could stop him.

"You know, dudes, you'd think finding a place down here would be easy," Michaelangelo said, strolling ahead. "But noooooo . . ." Mike's voice echoed down a deep hole as he suddenly crashed through the floor of the tunnel. His brothers kneeled at the edge of the hole to see if he was okay.

"Check it out!" Mike called from below. The brothers jumped to join him on an abandoned subway platform sealed in by rubble. A derailed subway car rotted on the rusty tracks.

"Roomy. Access to power and water," Donatello commented.

"It's well hidden," Leonardo approved.

Michaelangelo was not thrilled. "I hear the sewers in Connecticut are really nice."

Early the next morning, Professor Perry put down his stale coffee and ran a weary hand through his messy hair. It had been a long night keeping watch over the snarling, snapping new mutants. Several Foot were on hand as he finished making entries in his data log.

"How much longer?" Shredder demanded impatiently.

The weary professor snapped, "I don't know. It takes days."

"I want them as soon as possible," Shredder ordered, staring at the large, shadowy shapes banging the bars of their cages.

Perry looked at the fierce ninja guards and asked, "Aren't these enough for your vengeance?"

"The Foot have failed against the turtles. I have failed," Shredder said. "The next fight shall be freak against freak!"

In a dusty warehouse a black-clad Foot recruiter stood beside a pickpocket's dummy covered with tiny bells. With flying feet and fists Keno had defeated the other Foot hopefuls. He fearfully faced the final test for entry into the clan.

"Keno, wasn't it? You are the only one worthy of the final test. You have fifteen seconds. Remove as many bells as you can. One sound and you fail," the ninja instructed.

Keno swallowed hard. The ninja threw a dust bomb at the base of the dummy. Swirling smoke blinded Keno. "We work in concealment. Fifteen seconds. Go!"

Keno jumped into the dust cloud. But he was not alone. Raphael had followed him to the warehouse. Now the turtle secretly joined Keno in the thick smoke.

When the fifteen seconds had passed, the recruiter fanned away the smoke. Keno stood next to the dummy—and all the bells lay in a neat pile on the floor.

"Is this enough?" Keno smugly asked the stunned ninjas.

Behind a pile of boxes, Raph grinned. Their plan was working. With Keno in the clan, the turtles could find Foot headquarters.

Donatello adjusted a TV in the turtles new den. Freshly rigged with lighting

and straightened up a bit, it was still a long way from the cover of *Good Housekeeping*.

Leo descended the rope ladder hanging from the ceiling entrance. "There's no sign of Raph at the old Foot H.Q."

Michaelangelo stuck his head through the hole. "I reconned the TGRI waste site," he reported. "Zippo-alady-o, dudes."

Splinter and the others were disappointed until Mike said, "But look who came to visit!"

April O'Neil had arrived just in time to see her own news report on the newly fixed TV. She sat down with the turtles.

"I couldn't get much out of these guys," April said during the story about TGRI. Onscreen, workers carried equipment to trucks. The company press rep avoided April's questions and scoffed at the idea of mutations.

"I think they're shutting down," April concluded.

In the junkyard shack, Shredder turned to Tatsu.

"Open the cells!" he ordered.

The silent ninja hesitated. He stared at the heavy metal bars straining under the banging blows of two giant mutants.

"It's time they learned who their master is," Shredder stated. "Remove the bars and leave us."

Tatsu obeyed. He took one last fearful look at his master as Shredder braced for battle. Ripped from their hinges, the cage doors crashed to the floor. The hulking mutants stomped toward the awestruck Shredder.

"Wolf . . . snapping turtle . . . incredible!" Shredder gasped. "Attack if you will. When it is over, you will call me master!"

The monsters froze in their tracks.

Rahzar the wolf forced his hairy muzzle to shape the last word he heard. "Ma . . . ma . . . ma . . ."

The snapping turtle, Tokka, glared at

Shredder. "Mama?"

Inside his metal mask the ninja raised a puzzled eyebrow.

The beasts shuffled forward, hugged the shocked Shredder in their giant arms, and cried, "Mama! Mama!"

"Babies! They're babies!" Shredder shrieked in dismay.

"What did you expect?" Professor Perry asked. "They'd come out quoting *Macbeth*?"

The creatures sat on the floor playing with a thick steel pipe. Tokka whacked himself over the head to see how it felt while the proud professor examined Rahzar.

"They're stupid!" Shredder fumed furiously.

"They're not stupid. They're infants," Perry explained.

"They're stupid infants!" Shredder declared as Tokka bit the steel pipe in half, then banged the floor to splinters.

"Put that down!" Shredder scolded.

Tokka meekly obeyed.

"Fortunately, they think you're their mother," Perry said.

"They are of no use to me," Shredder complained. "Tatsu! See that these two 'things' are disposed of."

"You can't do that!" Perry cried. "They're living things."

"Not for long," said Shredder menacingly.

"Wait! Wait!" Perry shouted, and persuaded Shredder to watch a demonstration.

Soon Tokka and Rahzar were outside playing a merry game of catch with an old engine block. Bouncing between their giant arms, the massive metal motor seemed as light as a balloon. The professor explained that the mutants might not be intellectual giants, but they had other strengths—namely, strength!

Morning sun gleamed on heaps of rusting metal in the junkyard when Keno reported to the Foot recruiter. Other clan members were training in

PERSONALITY PROFILE

NAME: Rahzar
SPECIES: mutant wolf
PERSONALITY TRAITS: just a big baby
FAVORITE WEAPON: anything he can get his paws on
FAVORITE EXPRESSION: "Mama!"
FAVORITE FOOD: doughnuts
PET PEEVES: antimutagen cubes, seltzer, fleas

PERSONALITY PROFILE

NAME: Tokka
SPECIES: mutant snapping turtle
PERSONALITY TRAITS: incredibly infantile
FAVORITE WEAPON: his jaws
FAVORITE EXPRESSION: "Fun!"
FAVORITE FOOD: telephone poles
PET PEEVES: tight manholes, antimutagen cubes,
seltzer without lime

open areas between mounds of jumbled junk. Keno was told to get a training dogi from the shed.

As the teenager passed rows of scrap, he glimpsed Raphael in the rubble, moving alongside him. "First chance we get," Raph whispered, "we're outta here." The turtle stopped short. "I just saw a ghost!" he gasped. Out of the corner of his eye Raph saw . . . but it couldn't be! The metal mask of the Shredder! Keno and the turtle cautiously crept to the window of the sagging shack.

"Just what are you looking for?" Keno demanded as Raphael peered through the dirty window.

"Quiet! You wanna get us—" Raph warned, but it was too late! Tatsu and several Foot confronted the turtle and the teenager. Raphael was dismayed, but quickly bluffed, "Hi, guys! We were looking for a muffler for a '77 Chevy."

Tatsu motioned for the Foot to attack.

"Sheesh! Whatever happened to service with a smile?" Raphael joked, knocking down the first few of the Foot army.

Keno hurried to help the outnumbered turtle, but Raphael waved him away. "No sense both of us going down! Get outta here, kid. Tell the others!"

Reluctantly Keno obeyed. Fleeing on flying feet, the plucky teenager was pursued by two grim ninjas. Keno quickly flattened the Foot and with a last look at Raphael escaped to the safety of the street.

As Foot reinforcements piled on the half-shell hero, Raphael yelled, "I'm curious. Any of you guys ever heard the expression 'fair fight'?"

With that, a shadow fell over the brash, brave turtle. Raphael looked up and gasped, "Shredder!"

That night the brother turtles came to Shredder's lair to rescue Raphael, just as Shredder had planned. Keno had raced across the Brooklyn Bridge and through the maze of Manhattan to report Raphael's capture.

Under cover of darkness, the three ninja turtles peered from a junk pile into the central yard patrolled by a few Foot watchmen.

"Perimeter's quiet," whispered Donatello.

"A little too quiet," Leonardo said suspiciously.

They quickly dispatched the guards.

"That was easy," Don declared.

"A little too easy," observed Leo.

In the dim distance they could just make out the silhouette of a turtle tied to a stake.

UH-OHHH!

"Look! It's Raph!" Donatello exclaimed.

"A little too Raph," Michaelangelo joked.

Leo elbowed him. "Knock it off," he said. "Keep your eyes peeled. I don't like this."

The three turtles inched cautiously across the dark yard.

"You know? If they were gonna spring a trap," Donatello theorized, "they'd probably do it right about—"

A floodlight blinded the turtles, and with a sudden snap they were whisked up in a giant net. The tangled turtles swung above the ground in the glare.

"Nice call, Donnie!" Mike teased. "Pitifully late, but nice." The Foot swarmed beneath them and the floodlights glinted on the polished armor that could only

belong to . . .

"The Shred-Dude!" Michaelangelo exclaimed.

"I've been waiting for you," Shredder gloated. "I have a little surprise."

The crane arm holding their net swung the turtles closer to a bed of deadly ninja spikes rising in front of Raphael's stake.

"Bummer—turtle kabob!" Michaelangelo moaned.

Raphael struggled vainly against his bonds.

Shredder said, "Patience, Raphael. First them, then you. Drop them at my signal, Tatsu!"

The crane edged closer and closer to the deadly spikes.

"These nets are remarkably effective," Donatello observed. "Well constructed."

Michaelangelo stopped struggling long enough to joke, "Yeah, remind me to drop a note to Ralph Nader."

Just before the net reached the bed of spikes, an arrow whizzed through the air and severed the rope suspending the helpless turtles from the crane. The arrow quivered in Raphael's stake as the turtles dropped to safety.

Splinter stood high atop the tallest mound of junk, moonlight gleaming on his bow and glossy fur. "Cowabunga!" the ninja master murmured to himself.

"That's right, Shredder, you forgot we carry insurance," Leonardo said, freeing himself from the net.

"Mutual of Splinter, dude," crowed Michaelangelo.

"Get them!" Shredder cried. And the Foot flew into action.

Donatello ripped off the tape gagging Raphael's mouth.

"Yow! Why don't you just rip my lips off instead?" Raph griped. Don replaced the tape and went to work on Raphael's ropes.

Meanwhile, Leonardo and Michaelangelo easily defeated the Foot, using their own weapons and any loose junk on hand.

"These guys never were a challenge," Leo commented.

"This one's tired out." Mike laughed, knocking a ninja flat with an old tire.

The Foot continued to fall around the rampaging turtles. Raphael and Donatello joined the action. "Leave some for me!" Raphael demanded.

Michaelangelo smiled at his brother. "Hey, Raph, have a nice rest at Club Shred?"

Sensing defeat, Shredder could see it was time to play his aces. "Tokka! Rahzar!" he cried. An entire wall of the junk-

yard shack crashed down and out stepped the monstrous mutants in funky ninja armor. The turtles paused in surprise.

"What in the . . . ?" Leonardo marveled.

"Didn't I see these guys on *Wrestlemania*?" Mike wondered.

Shredder shouted, "Prove yourselves to me. Attack!" The snarling, snapping mutants rushed the stunned turtles.

Raphael growled defiantly, "The bigger they are . . ." And he took a running leap into Rahzar's massive chest. But he bounced off and fell on his shell.

"The more bones they break?" Mike asked his aching brother. Donatello's bo held Tokka at bay until the giant snapping turtle severed the staff with his powerful jaws. Tokka picked up the disarmed turtle and tossed him through the air. Donatello crashed into a toolshed and found himself sitting in the ruins beside Professor Perry.

"Hey, you're the TGRI guy!" Don exclaimed to the bound and gagged scientist. He ripped the tape off the professor's mouth.

"Ouch!" Perry yelped.

"I've gotta get the hang of that," Don muttered.

"Fun!" Rahzar bellowed, hurling Michaelangelo to the street.

Leo and Raph were receiving some "fun" of their own, while Mike happily discovered he had landed on a manhole.

"Guys! Over here!" Mike called, prying up the cover.

PERSONALITY PROFILE

NAME: Keno
PROFESSION: pizza delivery boy
PERSONALITY TRAITS: brave, bold, curious, and cocky
FAVORITE WEAPON: his hands and feet
FAVORITE EXPRESSION: "Hold the anchovies!"
FAVORITE FOOD: pizza, of course
PET PEEVES: low tippers, giant evil mutants, the Foot,
                   bad guys in general

PERSONALITY PROFILE

NAME: April O'Neil
FAVORITE COLOR: hot pink
PERSONALITY TRAITS: ambitious; has a soft spot
                           for hard news
FAVORITE WEAPON: microphone
FAVORITE EXPRESSION: "Give me a (news) break!"
FAVORITE FOOD: take-out Chinese
PET PEEVES: people who refuse to comment to the press

PERSONALITY PROFILE

NAME: Professor Jordan Perry
PROFESSION: mad scientist
PERSONALITY TRAITS: absent-minded genius; respects
                           all living things; long-winded
                           (and he talks too much, too)
FAVORITE WEAPON: his brain
FAVORITE EXPRESSION: "For every action there is an
                           equal and opposite reaction."
FAVORITE FOOD: pizza—isn't everyone's?
PET PEEVES: lost mutagen canisters, pushy villains

Leo and Raph hurried to join him, battling the beasts all the way. While Raph and Leo held off the monsters, Donatello and the professor climbed down to safety in the sewer.

"You go next," Leonardo told Raphael.

"No, you go next," proud Raphael argued.

"Okay, I'll tell you what," Leo agreed, then bumped his brother down the hole. "You go next." With a final flourish of his katana, the brave turtle leader leaped down.

"No! Stop them!" Shredder bellowed to his mutants.

Tokka plunged after the turtles, but the manhole was too small for his bulk.

The spiny snapping turtle plugged the hole as tight as a cork in a bottle.

"Tokka stuck," he sheepishly confessed to the fuming Shredder.

Safe beneath the struggling mutant, the turtles sighed with relief. Mike tickled Tokka's toes. "Itchy-kitchy-koo!"

Professor Perry stared at his rescuers. "Four turtles!"

"The guy's Ph.D. material, all right," Raphael sniped.

"Come on, we've got to join Splinter," Leo urged. He insisted that the professor close his eyes, so as not to give away their destination. With Mike guiding the professor, Leo led the limping turtles down the tunnel. Worse for wear, they

rubbed sore muscles all the way to the subway sanctuary.

Once they arrived at their destination, the professor gaped at the sight of Splinter and the turtles' ingenious den. The turtles were just as amazed that Perry knew about their oozy origin fifteen years before. In fact, he knew more about it than they did.

"You mean to say the formation of the ooze was all a big mistake?" Donatello asked in disbelief.

"Donatello, I think your name was, right?" Perry asked, leaning back in his makeshift chair. "You see, an unknown mixture of discarded chemicals was accidentally exposed to a series of radiative waves. The resulting 'ooze,' as you put it, was found to have remarkable and dangerous mutanagenic properties."

"Huh?" Mike grunted.

"Big mistake," Raph interpreted.

"Please continue, Professor," Splinter said.

Perry told them that as TGRI employees hurried to dispose of the dangerous mixture their truck crashed, and one of the canisters rolled down the sewer. The turtles all knew the rest.

Donatello was upset by the professor's explanation. He stepped away to brood by himself. Splinter watched him.

"What troubles you, my son?" Splinter asked gently.

"I just always thought there'd be more to the ooze. You know, to us," Don explained. Leo placed a hand on Donatello's shoulder.

"Do not confuse the specter of your origin with your present worth, my son," Splinter gently reassured the troubled turtle.

Don said, "I just don't believe him. There's got to be more to it."

The brothers turned to their teacher.

Splinter twitched his whiskers thoughtfully. "The search for a beginning rarely has so easy an end. But our search will wait. Tonight's encounter has left us with larger problems."

On a quiet secluded street a truck's tarp peeled back and Tokka and Rahzar got their first look at the city. The monstrous mutants squinted at the bright street lamps.

"Go! Play! Have fun!" Shredder instructed, and the beasts bounded happily into the street.

"Master say have fun," Rahzar burbled, his huge hairy paws ripping down a street lamp.

Tokka spit out the shattered remains of a telephone pole to shout, "Fun!"

Entering a taxi, an elderly couple peered at the path of destruction. Street lamps winked out one by one.

"Sophie, look!" the old man cried. "There's some animals knocking down telephone poles!"

"Let them get their own cab," Sophie said with a sigh.

Police puzzled over the tangled mess of wires, poles, and lampposts littering the street the next morning. April and her crew wrapped up an interview with Chief Sterns, who was as brusque and evasive as ever. Unsatisfied, April chased after the chubby chief with a few off-the-record questions.

"Miss O'Neil, my record on the record clearly shows I have no off-the-record record," Sterns blustered suspiciously.

"Were there any large tooth and claw marks found on the scene?" April persisted.

"How did you know—" Sterns caught himself. "That I don't know what you're talking about?"

April told the chief she thought the damage was caused by two "really big animals," but he refused to believe her. When she warned that there were two

dangerous "things" out there, Sterns wondered aloud what he could do about it. April shuddered, realizing that the grouchy chief was right—what *could* the police do?

"I guess you're not the ones to handle it." April shrugged.

"That's what we do best," Chief Sterns said sarcastically.

Frustrated, April went back to her crew. Then she noticed Freddy was missing. Another crew member told her Freddy had gone home sick. So April went to the equipment van herself. But before she could get anything from it, she was dragged into an alley by black-gloved hands.

"Hello, April," said a sinister member of the Foot.

"Freddy!" April recognized the man in the black dogi.

"Our master has a message for your friends," Freddy said.

"And if you don't go to this construction site tonight, he'll send Tokka and Rahzar into Central Park," April later told the turtles in their subway den. She was still breathless from her encounter with Freddy and the other Foot.

Donatello gasped. "All those people!"

"There is no choice but to meet Shredder as he wishes," Splinter concluded. They were being forced to fight the mutant monsters again—even before their bruises could heal.

April was near tears. "You guys don't have a chance!"

"There's no other way," Raphael said quietly.

"Wait!" Professor Perry exclaimed. "There might be a way."

Perry percolated a plan. They enlisted Keno, who picked up a weird array of chemicals—and a few pizza pies—and brought the stuff over. The turtles were soon stirring a batch of foul-smelling goop under Perry's direction.

"Michaelangelo, hand me more dimethylchlorinide."

Mike stared at a row of chemicals. "Uhhhh . . ."

"The pink bottle," the professor said.

"Are you sure this stuff'll work?" Raphael asked.

"I contaminated the ooze used to

transform Rahzar and Tokka to make them less intelligent—and therefore less dangerous. I had no idea I would later formulate an antimutagen based on that contamination," the professor fretted.

"Huh?" Michaelangelo was confused.

"He's not sure," Raph translated.

"Can it hurt us?" wondered Leonardo.

"The formula is keyed to the specific physiological weaknesses induced by the contaminated ooze," Perry replied.

Michaelangelo simply looked at Raphael, who said, "It can't hurt us." Mike mouthed a silent "Oh" and ate his pizza.

The professor ladled lumpy goop into a glass held by Leo.

"So all we have to do is spray them with this?" Don asked.

Professor Perry swallowed. "I'm afraid ingestion is the only course."

Raph, Leo, and Don grunted in unanimous confusion. "Huh?"

Around a mouthful of pizza, Michaelangelo said, "They have to eat it." The others looked at Mike in astonishment.

"Affirma—" The professor corrected himself. "Yo, my man."

"Great." Leonardo sniffed the ugly goo. "Sounds easy."

"We could solidify it in ice cube trays," Don suggested.

"Well, I've got an idea," Mike offered his dubious brothers.

In a few hours the turtles stood mask to mask with Shredder in the dockside construction site swarming with the Foot.

"How ironic. The very thing that was your making will now be your undoing," Shredder gloated, brandishing a TGRI canister in the floodlights. "Let the games begin!"

"All we need is *Wide World of Sports*

and a blimp," Mike said as Tokka and Rahzar advanced with earthshaking steps.

"Wait!" Leo called. "First we should observe the ancient ritual of the prefight doughnut." Mike held out a box, and Rahzar happily selected a doughnut. Before he popped it into his giant jaws, his nose crinkled at the smell of the brown cube in the doughnut's center. The angry monster slapped the box from Mike's hands and squeezed the turtle. Tokka crushed Leonardo as Shredder shrieked, "Kill them!"

"We should've bought muffins," Mike choked. The mutants hurled Leo and Mike into their brothers. They all landed in a clump of shells and bruises.

"Plan B?" Leonardo suggested.

"No, let's do the doughnut thing again," Raph sneered.

The turtles escaped the flailing fists of the monster mutants. Mike scrambled onto Leo's shoulders; Don onto Raph's. The confused mutants swung at the topmost turtles, who bobbed and ducked while loading slingshots with a double dose of antimutagen cubes. Leo and Raph punched the beasts' bellies as hard as they could. The mutants' mouths opened and Don and Mike scored two direct hits with the cubes.

Tokka and Rahzar swallowed, slowed, and wobbled slightly.

"It's working!" Donatello cried happily.

But the beasts merely belched. They patted their tummies and resumed their attack. The turtles backed away.

"Man, ugly *and* impolite!" Michaelangelo said.

"That's it?" Raphael asked. "Now what? We don't have a Plan C. I knew we shouldn't have trusted that professor guy."

Tokka and Rahzar's savage pursuit forced the turtles to retreat to the docks. Leo and Raph crashed through the doors of the Dockside Club, landing in the center of its busy dance floor. The band bopped and the jaunty rapper onstage never stopped. The hip audience applauded the newcomers' funky "costumes." Backstage, a puzzled promoter wondered where the extras came from.

Michaelangelo and Donatello crashed through a wall and onto the jumping dance floor, followed by the raging Rahzar.

"Hey, check it out. This place is rocking," Mike said.

"Great! Now we can get pulverized to a beat," said Don.

Donatello spotted Professor Perry at the front door.

"Professor!" Don cried as Rahzar flung a chair at the absent-minded scientist. Donatello tackled Perry to protect him just in time.

"It would appear that the antimutagen has been somewhat ineffective," Perry observed mildly as he and Don crawled to cover behind the bar.

Leo and Raph tried to tame Tokka with whatever they found on hand. But the giant snapping turtle chomped chairs, trashed tables, and kept on coming!

"There's a bright side to this," Leo said. "It can't get any worse." Just then, Tatsu led a legion of Foot into the club.

Huddled beneath the bar, Donatello and the professor put their heads together.

"Carbon dioxide is essential to the antimutagenic process. Their burping probably retarded the reaction," Perry theorized.

"Isn't there a way to speed it back up?" Don asked.

"The reintroduction of CO_2 could act as a catalyst," the professor explained. "The problem is finding a ready supply."

Just as they put on their thinking caps, Don and Perry spotted seltzer bottles under the bar.

Meanwhile, Keno had been meditating with Splinter in the subway den.

"We should be out there with the guys!" Keno finally exploded.

Splinter said, "You have youth. I have experience. Only those who now fight have both."

"I can fight," Keno argued.

"Fighting is the last choice of the true ninja. Used unwisely it is a double-edged sword," the ancient rat said.

"You can't keep me here," Keno declared impatiently.

"No, I can't," Splinter agreed.

Back at the Dockside Club, the turtles were tired of fighting. They had kept the Foot at bay while battling the tireless Tokka and Rahzar.

Leonardo was skeptical of the seltzer plan.

"Just do it!" Donatello shouted, aiming a bottle.

Mike and Raph jumped on the backs of the bucking monster mutants and held on for dear life as they pried open their huge jaws. Don and Leo sprayed seltzer, getting as much on their brothers as they got in the mutants' mouths.

Rahzar and Tokka shook off the turtle riders, then froze in their tracks. They grabbed their stomachs.

"Tummy . . ." Rahzar groaned.

"Ache . . ." Tokka moaned. And the two mutants fell backward into the waiting arms of Mike and Raph, who lowered the now-sleeping giants to the floor

as they shrank to normal size.

"These dudes are copping major Z's," Mike marveled.

"Good! Now let's have some fun," Leonardo said, confidently facing the remaining Foot. The audience applauded. Backstage the promoter brushed his assistant aside. "Forget calling the police. They like it!"

As the fierce fight spilled onto the stage, the band took it in stride. Music blended with battle cries. The rapper improvised. "Well, it looks kinda weird, but it's plain t'be seen. The bad guys wear black, and the good guys be green!"

The turtles made short work of the Foot onstage. The audience went wild as the turtles timed their blows to the beat. Tatsu was the last to fall, as audience and band shouted, "Ninja Rap!" The turtles took a bow, but the show wasn't over.

Knocking down a huge speaker,

Shredder made a grand entrance. "The battle is yours, but the war is far from over," he snarled. "Not so long as I possess this canister!"

"Hand it over, Shredder," Raphael demanded.

"Of course! In small doses, through future mutants," Shredder threatened even as the turtles surrounded him.

But just as they tensed to attack, Keno burst in.

"Hold on, guys! I'm coming," he cried, and leaped into the fray, foiling the turtles' careful plan.

In the ensuing confusion the canister rolled offstage past the stunned dancers and was picked up by Professor Perry.

"Farewell, my friends," he said as he left the club.

Desperate to escape, Shredder grabbed a dancer and backed her against a mammoth speaker.

"If you try to stop me, I'll cover her with this!" he shouted, plucking a vial of glowing ooze from his robes. "Did you think I'd be foolish enough to keep it all in one place?"

"Well, sort of," Leonardo admitted as he and Raph backed reluctantly away.

On Don's signal Mike snatched up an electric guitar, Keno leaped to grab the girl, and Don cranked an amplifier to maximum. Michaelangelo stroked the guitar strings and the speaker exploded with a thunderous E chord. Shredder was blasted through a window and splashed in the river beyond.

"Rock-'n'-roll!" Mike cheered.

The turtles took off after Shredder.

Keno and the shaken girl sat up on the floor where they had landed. At first she was so scared she was angry.

"Man, who are you barging in here, yelling like the kung fu goddess of . . ." Then she remembered Keno had saved her. Besides, he was cute! She offered her hand. "Name's Jack."

"You mean like in Jackie?" Keno asked.

"I mean like in *Jack,*" she snapped.

"Keno." The starry-eyed teenager smiled. She was cute! "Do you like pizza?"

On the damp docks the turtles searched for signs of Shredder. Finding none, they shouted, "Cowabunga!" with enthusiastic high-threes.

Then an enormous shadow darkened the dock. Uh-oh! A dripping mutant behemoth towered above the water, its hulking body bulging from torn and split ninja armor: SuperShredder!

"That last vial of ooze!" Leonardo exclaimed.

Antimutagen cubes would be useless, since this was the pure, uncontaminated ooze. SuperShredder swung a steel gir-

der plucked from a pile of nearby construction supplies. Not only was he big, he was amazingly fast. He whacked manhole-sized chunks out of the dock as the turtles dodged and ducked.

The turtles' weapons were useless! The green foursome were tossed to the dock's lower level, where they swiftly sought shelter.

"Any ideas?" Leonardo frantically asked.

Mike stared out to sea. "How far is it to England?"

The turtles were forced to retreat through the maze of crisscrossed wooden supports under the dock. SuperShredder followed, smashing the supports with his powerful blows. The dock creaked and shuddered under the relentless attacks.

"This isn't gonna take much more!" Donatello warned.

"Shredder! Listen to me. You'll kill us all!" Leo cried.

SuperShredder smiled. "Then so be it." His ghastly voice boomed, and he continued his savage splintering of the few remaining beams. A cement mixer plunged through the weakened dock and splashed in the river below.

"It's coming down!" Raphael yelled.

"We're pancakes!" Michaelangelo was turtle-ly freaked.

"No!" Leonardo denied above the din of destruction. "The true ninja is a master of his environment and himself. Don't forget"—he pointed to a hole at their feet—"we're turtles!"

As Leo leaped through the hole, the dock caved in with a thunderous roar. Construction material and debris rained down, crushing everything in its path.

Then all fell silent above the jumbled heap of girders, bricks, and broken wooden beams. Nothing could have survived.

But a shell bobbed to the river's surface. Then another, and another, until all four turtles scrambled onto the ruins.

Michaelangelo sighed. "I've said it before and I'll say it again . . ." His brothers joined him. *"I love being a turtle!"*

"Too bad Shredder can't say the same," Raphael said.

A pile of bricks trembled and tumbled away from a huge arm with bent ninja spikes rising from the rubble.

"Nobody could have survived that!" Raphael insisted.

The hand faltered and fell limp.

"Not even the Shredder," Leonardo said somberly.

That night on the news April wrapped up her studio report.

"And in a bizarre final note to the mysterious disappearance of TGRI, this message was delivered to the station earlier today: 'To Leonardo, Donatello, Michaelangelo, and Raphael: Thanks for your help, dudes. Signed, Professor Jordan Perry.'"

April grinned into the camera. "Of course, we can only guess its meaning. And now this . . ."

Splinter turned off the TV and put down his remote control as the Teenage Mutant Ninja Turtles happily climbed down the rope ladder to their lair. They searched for the right words to congratulate themselves on a job well done.

"Cowabunga says it all, dudes!" Michaelangelo declared.

The turtles high- and low-threed. Splinter quietly examined a newspaper as the turtle brothers gathered around their master.

"Were you seen?" Splinter softly asked.

"Of course not, Master Splinter," Leonardo replied.

"We practice ninja," Donatello elaborated.

"The art of invisibility," Michaelangelo finished.

Splinter held up the newspaper. On the front page was a large photo of the turtles onstage at the Dockside Club.

NINJA RAP IS BORN! the headline screamed.

"Practice harder," Splinter said.